Puffin Books

THE CABBAGE PATCH WAR

'You can't have a party without music,' said Dad.
'You can't have a fire without smoke,' said Whacka.

It went from bad to worse after that.
A barbecue from hell. Spuds on the roof.
A visit from the police.
It was war, a fight to the finish between
Dad and Whacka.
And Chris was right in the middle of it.

All because Dad vomited in the cabbage patch.

It could only be a Paul Jennings story.

And it is.

Other books by Paul Jennings

THE CABBAGE PATCH WAR

Paul Jennings

Illustrated by Craig Smith

PUFFIN BOOKS

Puffin Books
Penguin Books Australia Ltd
487 Maroondah Highway, PO Box 257
Ringwood, Victoria 3134, Australia
Penguin Books Ltd
Harmondsworth, Middlesex, England
Viking Penguin, A Division of Penguin Books USA Inc.
375 Hudson Street, New York, New York 10014, USA
Penguin Books Canada Limited
10 Alcorn Avenue, Toronto, Ontario, Canada M4V 3B2
Penguin Books (N.Z.) Ltd
182–190 Wairau Road, Auckland 10, New Zealand

First published by Penguin Books Australia, 1996

10 9 8 7 6 5 4 3 2 1

Typeset in Palatino by Midland Typesetters, Maryborough, Victoria
Made and printed in Australia by Australian Print Group, Maryborough, Victoria

National Library of Australia
Cataloguing-in-Publication data:

Jennings, Paul, 1943– .
The cabbage patch war

ISBN 0 14 038243 7

I. Smith, Craig, 1955– . II. Title

A823.3

For Kyle and Sage
P.J.

For Bruno and his dad
C.S.

1

My brother Chris is
still only eight
years old.
Which is rather
young to go to
war. Well, 'go to
war' is probably
not quite the way
to put it. But there
was a battle.
And Chris was
right in the middle
of it, that's for
certain.

It all started at lunch time. The whole eight of us –
six kids and Mum and Dad – were sitting at the table
looking at something awful. Dad gave a big smile. 'I
bought six dozen oysters,' he said. 'That's seventy-
two all together.' He nodded at me. 'So how many
do we get each?'

Dad is always giving us little sums to do in our heads. It drives me crazy. 'I know,' said Sky. 'None. They are disgusting. I'm not touching them.'

'Okay,' said Dad. 'Seventy-two divided by seven. That makes ten each and two left over. I'd better eat the last two – just to be fair.'

'None for me, thanks,' I said.

'Me neither,' said Hayden. 'Revolting.'

'They are foul,' said Julie. 'Nearly as bad as cabbage.' She put a finger in her mouth pretending to make herself sick.

'Yuck, yuck, yuck,' said Chris.

'Jack is too young for oysters,' said Mum. 'And you know that I don't like them, dear.'

Dad looked a bit hurt. But only for a second.

4

'Okay,' he said. 'I'll just have to eat them all myself.'

And he did.

We sat there and watched while Dad shovelled in all those oysters. It was a horrible sight. But there was a reason for it.

Poor Dad had an eating problem. It began the day he dug out the cabbages and put in onions. The onions died so he tried cabbages again. But they just wouldn't grow. It almost seemed as if the garden was mad at him. Only one little cabbage was still alive.

Dad was so sad. 'Growing cabbages is my hobby,' he said. 'I've lost my touch. I'm a failure.'

So he turned to eating junk food instead. Pizza, hamburgers, prawns, trifle, chips. You name it and he ate it.

Beer, too. He loved his beer. On a warm summer's evening he would sit in the backyard with a beer in his hand and stare at the dead vegetable patch. It was a very sad sight. Sometimes he would give his big beer belly a pat. Just to make himself feel better.

Anyway, to get back to the oysters. Dad shovelled about fifty of them into his mouth without stopping. Then he started to slow down. 'That's enough, dear,' said Mum. 'You'll make yourself ill.'

But Dad kept going. Slower and slower. We all watched in silence. Something bad was going to happen. I just knew it was. Finally Dad stopped eating. There was only one oyster left.

'Don't eat it, Dad,' I said. 'Give up.'

'Oh, foul,' yelled Sky.

'Revolting,' said Hayden.

'Yuck, yuck, yuck,' said Chris.

'Give up, dear,' said Mum. 'You know you've had enough.'

'He feels sick,' chuckled Julie. 'What a wimp.'

Dad glared around the table. 'Wimp, am I? I'll show you.'

He slowly lifted the last oyster to his mouth. His face was a bit green. He didn't look too good. He put the oyster in his mouth and closed his lips.

'He hasn't swallowed it,' shouted Chris.
'It's still in his mouth.
He can't get it down.'

Dad gave him a stubborn look. And swallowed. For a moment nothing happened. Then his eyes started to bulge. His stomach rumbled. Suddenly he jumped to his feet and ran outside. A terrible retching, splashing noise floated in through the window. The sound mixed with the laughter from inside. Dad was as sick as a dog.

2

All the kids went outside to look at the vomit.

Seventy-two oysters, beer and bits of red and green stuff do not make a pretty sight. Especially when they have been chewed up and swallowed first.

None of the kids would clean it up. Neither would Mum. 'The hog always returns to its own vomit,' she said.

Everyone felt a bit ill. Except Dad. He scooped the sick up on a shovel and dug it in around the tiny cabbage. 'Good fertiliser,' he said with a grin.

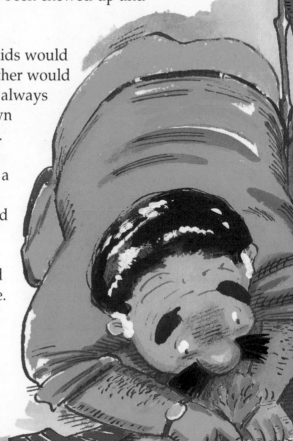

It was good
fertiliser, too.
That cabbage grew
to a huge size
within a month.

Dad watered it every
night. He loved that cabbage. Anyone would have
thought that it was a person. He patted it and loved
it just like a baby. He didn't feel like a failure any
more. Everything was good.

Until . . .

The beginning of the war.

See, Dad decided to have a barbecue. But he didn't invite our neighbour, Whacka. I was a bit upset because his daughter Robyn was my best friend. 'I want Robyn to come,' I said.

'It's only for the cricket club,' said Dad. 'Whacka can't play cricket for nuts.'

The day of the barbecue arrived. The new gas barbecue was fired up. The first stubby was opened. The first sausage started to sizzle. There was a lot of laughing and joking. The CD was pumping out Dad's old Irish music. The sun was shining. Perfect (except that Robyn wasn't there).

And then it happened.

SMOKE.

Not nice barbecue smoke. Stinking, swirling smoke coming from over the fence. Everyone started to cough and choke and rub their eyes. It was terrible. The smoke was so thick that it blotted out the sun. 'Strike,' yelled Dad. 'Where's that coming from?'

He tried to pull himself up to peer over the fence but he couldn't quite manage it. His beer pot was bigger than ever. He grabbed a chair and stood on it. Then he peered down into Whacka's garden.

'Geeze,' said Dad. 'Whacka's having a burn-off. Today of all days.'

Chris scrambled up and sat on the fence with him. Whacka was setting fire to old tyres, grass and green branches that he had cut from his trees.

'Hey, Whacka,' yelled Dad. 'Cut it out. We're having a barbie over here.'

'Yeah,' said Chris. 'We're having a barbie.'

'I know you are,' said Whacka. 'You can hear it from miles away. Why don't you turn that music down? It's a terrible racket.'

'You can't have a party without music,' said Dad.

'And you can't have fire without smoke,' said Whacka.

Dad glared over the fence. 'Put out that fire.'

'You turn off that music.'

'Never,' said Dad.

'Get nicked, then,' yelled Whacka through the smoke. He threw another branch on the fire with an evil chuckle. Whacka had a very mean laugh. He also had a beer gut that was just as bad as Dad's. In fact Whacka and Dad had the biggest beer bellies in the district.

Suddenly Dad grinned to himself. Then he rushed across the garden and fetched the hose. He fixed a sprinkler to the end – the sort that you can adjust to spray wherever you want. He set it on the ground and turned on the tap.

'Get him, Dad,' yelled Chris.

He is so immature, is Chris.

'I will, son. I will,' said Dad. A huge jet of water shot up over the fence and fizzed down onto the fire. In no time at all the fire was out. Dad looked like a general who had just won a huge battle. He was very happy with what he had done.

3

Dad stood back and smiled his wonderful smile. He had great teeth. They were his best asset and he was very proud of them. They were so white that they shone through his moustache like the moon rising behind some bushes.

The guys in the cricket club all laughed at Dad squirting the water over the fence. They yelled and shouted and drank more stubbies.

'I told you to invite
Whacka,' said Mum. 'He's
annoyed because you didn't ask him to the barbie.'

'He's a ratbag,' said Dad.

'Well, he's upset,' said Mum. 'And you can't really
blame him.'

I peered over the fence. 'He's even more upset
now,' I said.

Whacka was out for revenge. He ran towards us.
'I'm getting out of here,' Chris yelled. He
jumped down and ran for it. Just in time.

There was an angry roar from the
other side of the fence. Whacka's red
face appeared. He pointed something
over the fence. It was a nozzle – of a hose.

Suddenly a great flood of water poured over the fence. It hit Dad right on the chest. The pressure was so strong that it nearly knocked him over.

'You bludger,' yelled Dad. He grabbed his own hose and started squirting Whacka. They stood there like two ancient gunfighters from the wild west. I couldn't believe it. It was a shoot-out with hoses. They were both soaked to the skin in a matter of seconds. The guys in the cricket team yelled and shouted louder than ever. They all barracked for Dad of course. They were so childish. The whole lot of them.

Even Googly Shaw, the captain, had to have his

say. 'Go, Johnny boy.'

'Hit him for a six.'

'Bowl him for a duck.'

A great whoosh of water
hit Whacka fair in the face.

'He is a duck,' someone
yelled.

'Yahoo,' shouted Chris.
'Cop that.'

The guys in the cricket team and
their wives rolled around laughing. But not for long.

Whacka was as angry as a wasp in a bottle. He turned the hose on the guests. 'See if you think this is funny,' he yelled.

Everyone was soaked. We all turned and ran for the house. But Dad and Whacka just stood there squirting each other with the water. Chris jumped around like a water spirit, egging Dad on. Soon the garden was awash. All the chairs and tables were drenched and strewn about. The steak and sausages were all swept off the barbie onto the patio. 'This is terrible,' I said.

'A wash-out,' said Julie.

'A bun-fight,' said Sky.

'Revolting,' said Hayden.

'Fantastic,' said Chris.

'A disaster,' said Mum. 'A total disaster.' Little Jack didn't say anything at all. He was asleep in his high-chair.

The soaking-wet guests started to leave. 'The barbecue from hell,' Chris heard Slogger Stevens' wife say as she jumped into their car.

In the end, Whacka's wife Anne turned off his hose. Mum did the same to Dad. Then she dragged him inside. She gave Dad the biggest lecture ever. 'Stupid behaviour,' she snapped. 'What an example to set for the children.'

'Good on ya, Dad,' Chris said. 'You showed the ratbag a thing or two.'

'You're both immature,' I said.

Mum looked at Dad and wagged a finger. 'I want this to be the end of the matter,' she told him in a very stern voice.

That's what she wanted.

But it wasn't what she got.

The next morning, Dad went out into the garden. There was a terrible scream. 'It's gone,' he shrieked. 'It's gone.'

We all rushed outside. 'What's gone?' asked Mum.

'The cabbage. Someone's taken it.'

'Good,' said Julie. 'I hate cabbage.'

Dad glared at the kids angrily.

'It wasn't me,' I said.

'Nor me.'

'Nor me.'

'Nor me.'

'And it certainly wasn't Jack,' said Mum. 'He can't even walk yet.'

'Look,' yelled Chris. 'Footprints.'

Dad looked at the fence. 'Whacka,' screamed Dad. 'Whacka has nicked my cabbage. He wants revenge.'

Dad scrambled up the fence and jumped over.
Chris followed.

They were gone for a long time. When they came
back Dad was red in the face. He stomped into the
kitchen and helped himself to five meat pies. Then
he ate seven lamingtons one after the other. Things
were looking bad.

'What happened?' I said to Chris.

'Whacka said he didn't steal the cabbage.
Dad called him a liar. So Whacka
slammed the door in Dad's face.
The war is getting worse.'

'That's silly,' I said to Chris. I went
inside to discuss it with Dad but he
wouldn't listen to anyone.
'Dad,' I said, 'Robyn is
my best friend. And
she's his daughter.'

'Too bad,' said Dad.
'I'm having nothing
to do with cabbage
thieves. And
that's that.'

4

Several days passed and all was calm. If Dad and Whacka passed each other in the street they both looked the other way. But Mum and Whacka's wife Anne just talked to each other as if nothing had happened. So did Robyn and I. Best friends don't break up just because their fathers are crazy.

Then Whacka bought a new dog. A big old thing called Bitsa. 'Bitsa this and bitsa that,' said Dad. 'A mongrel. Like Whacka.'

Chris liked Bitsa. But seeing as how it was the dog of the enemy Chris couldn't really go over the fence and pat it.

The real trouble started the next night. Bitsa barked and barked. Every time a possum came out of a tree Bitsa would start barking.

Dad roamed around the house. The slightest whimper would get him out of bed. 'Ruddy dog,' he said. 'Whacka's doing it on purpose. He's put the dog kennel right down the back of his yard near our place. We get disturbed and he doesn't. Well, I'm not standing for it.'

Later that night I was woken up by Chris sneaking out of his bed. 'Where are you going?' I said.

Chris held a finger up to his lips. 'Go back to your bed,' he said. 'We have work to do.' I followed him outside and found Dad in the backyard.

'What are you up to?' I asked.

'Shh,' Dad said. 'We don't want your mother finding out what's going on.' He was carrying a sack in one hand.

'Have you got the ammo?' said Chris.

Dad nodded. He reached into the sack and pulled out a large potato. 'If I have to stay awake at night then Whacka does too,' he said. Dad threw back his arm and then hurled the potato into the air.

Dad is a very good bowler. He once took eight wickets for three runs. He never misses.

The potato landed with an enormous thump on Whacka's tin roof. Then it began to roll down. 'Whumpa, whumpa, whumpa, whumpa.' It's amazing how much noise a spud can make on a tin roof in the middle of the night. The potato came to a stop in Whacka's spouting.

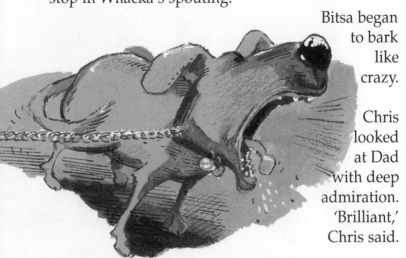

Bitsa began to bark like crazy.

Chris looked at Dad with deep admiration. 'Brilliant,' Chris said.

They really were childish. Both of them.

At that moment the windows in Whacka's house filled with light. His back door opened and Whacka came out into the yard dressed in his pyjamas. He stared up into the trees. He didn't know what had made the noise. Dad tried not to laugh. 'He thinks it's a possum,' he said.

We crept back inside. 'Don't turn on the lights,' said Dad. 'Or he'll know it's us. From now on, if Bitsa wakes me up, I wake Whacka up.' Dad put an arm around my shoulder. 'Don't tell your mother,' he said. 'She wouldn't understand.'

'I don't understand either,' I said. 'Whacka and his family are our friends.'

'Enemies,' said Chris. 'Don't forget the cabbage.'

Every night for the next week Dad and Chris crept into the backyard and threw potatoes onto Whacka's roof. Whacka kept running out with a torch and searching everywhere but he didn't see the potatoes because they were stuck in his spouting. In the end he climbed onto the roof and found all the spuds up there. 'Right,' he yelled into the dark night. 'It's war, is it. You'll be sorry for this, Johnny boy.'

Two nights later Whacka had a party with the Rotary Club. The noise was terrible. Much worse than our washed-out barbecue. But Dad decided not to throw any more spuds. 'Not now he's onto us,' he said.

The next morning Dad went to get the mail and discovered that someone had vomited into the letter-box. It was all over the letters and Dad had to wipe them clean. 'It was Whacka,' said Dad. 'He never could hold his oysters. I'll get him for this.'

'Yes,' yelled Chris. 'I can think of something to do in their letter-box.'

'No,' said Dad. 'Better not.'

Well, it just went from bad to worse after that. Whacka let down Dad's tyres. Dad rang Whacka up at three in the morning and told him off. Whacka lit a fire every time we went into the backyard. Dad rigged his stereo speakers up on the garage wall facing Whacka's windows. Then he put on one of my CDs and turned the volume up full in the middle of the night. He patted me on the head. 'That'll fix him,' said Dad. 'It's the worst music I've ever heard.'

'Thanks very much,' I said.

Just then there was a knock on the door. It was a policeman holding a notebook. 'You can't have music that loud,' he said. 'You're keeping the whole neighbourhood awake.'

'That's the idea,' said Chris. 'It's a war.'

Mum pulled Chris inside and I rushed over and turned off the music. Dad shut the door so that Mum couldn't hear what was said. After a bit Dad came inside holding a pink piece of paper.

Mum snatched it from his hand. She was furious. 'A two-hundred-dollar fine. For a stupid argument. This has got to stop,' she said. 'I can't live here with all this going on. If you and Whacka can't make friends we'll have to move.'

There was dead silence.

'You couldn't,' I said.

'Yes I could,' said Mum.

And she meant it.

5

Well, the last and worst trick came about two weeks later. It was over the apple tree. It was huge and old. Every year it grew hundreds of delicious apples. The only problem was, half of the branches hung over into Whacka's yard. Normally Dad let Whacka pick the ones on his side.

'Not this year,' said Dad. 'No way. You shin up the tree, Chris, and pick all the apples on Whacka's side before he can get them.'

'That's not fair, Dad,' I said.

'Whose side are you on anyway?' said Chris. He quickly climbed up the tree and started picking. He had to really stretch out for the ones on Whacka's side.

'Careful,' said Dad. 'We don't want you falling into his garden.'

Chris hurried as quickly as he could. If Whacka came out it would mean big trouble.

Soon there were only a few apples left on the furthest branches. 'Chris can't reach,' I said. 'Tell him to come down.'

'Okay,' said Dad. 'I'll do it myself.'

Chris scrambled down and Dad struggled up into the tree and started picking. He had quite a hard time of it because his big beer gut kept getting in the way. He was just reaching out for the last apple when a furious voice roared from the other side of the fence.

'Get back over your own side,' shouted Whacka.

'They're my apples,' said Dad.

'Like fun they are. The ones on my side are mine,' said Whacka. 'Give them back.'

Dad grinned triumphantly and flashed those brilliant teeth in a gloating smile. He shook his head. 'Make me,' he said.

Whacka was really upset. You could see veins on his head starting to throb. He raced back inside and came back with a saw. 'I don't want these branches hanging over my garden,' he said. 'I think I'll remove them. Then I'll burn them off.' He started to saw away at a lower branch.

Dad leaned down. Quick as a flash he snatched the saw out of Whacka's hand. Then threw the saw down to Chris. It was amazing. I still don't know how he managed it.

'You ratbag,' screamed Whacka. He grabbed the end of the half-sawn branch and started pulling on it. He bent it back and back and back but it wouldn't break. Dad leaned down and mocked him. 'Weak,' said Dad.

Whether his hands slipped or whether he did it on purpose I couldn't say. But Whacka let go of the branch and it whipped back and slashed into Dad's face.

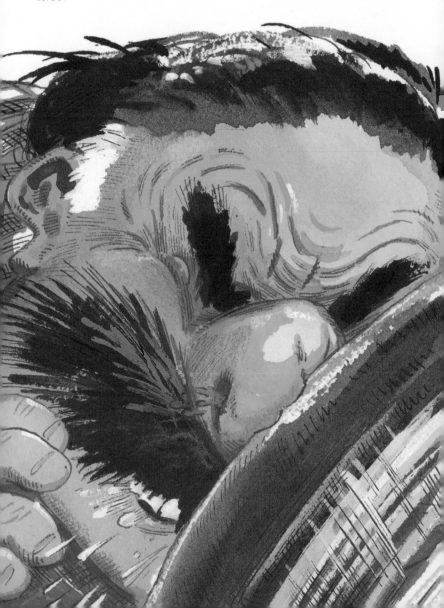

Dad screamed and fell crashing down into Whacka's yard. Chris scrambled over the fence and looked at Dad. He was lying there moaning and groaning. There was blood and broken teeth all over his face.

'Geeze, I'm sorry mate,' said Whacka. He looked as if he meant it, too. Whacka tried to help but Dad pushed him away. Chris pulled Dad to his feet and helped him stagger back home.

6

Well, Dad was in hospital for three days. He had a fractured jaw and lost ten of his front teeth. 'There's nothing I can do,' said the dentist. 'They all have to come out.' Then she uttered the fateful words. 'It's false teeth for you, I'm afraid.'

Dad groaned and hung his head in his hands. For a moment I thought he was going to cry. He had just lost his best asset.

'We'll get him for this,' said Chris.

'No you won't,' said Mum.

Things went quiet for a whole month. Dad and Chris played no tricks and neither did Whacka.

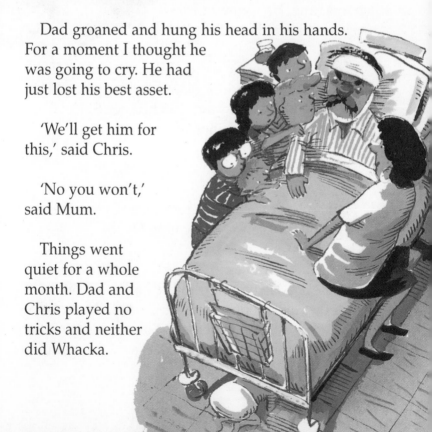

It was the calm before the storm.

The day Dad came home with his false teeth was the beginning of the end of the nightmare. Dad stared into the mirror. 'Look at them,' he said. 'They're phoney. Anyone can tell that they're false. And they hurt. And food gets under them. And they click and clack when I talk. That Whacka is going to suffer for this. I'm really going to fix him up this time. He's going to wish he'd never been born.'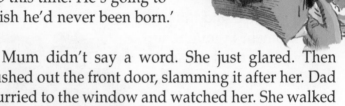

Mum didn't say a word. She just glared. Then rushed out the front door, slamming it after her. Dad hurried to the window and watched her. She walked straight into Whacka's house.

'Talking with the enemy,' said Dad.

Half an hour later Mum returned. 'Get undressed and get on the scales,' she said to Dad.

'What . . .?' he began. Then he saw the look in Mum's eyes. He went up to the bathroom, took off his clothes and stepped onto the scales. 'Ninety-five kilos,' said Mum. 'Exactly the same as Whacka. You're both terribly overweight. It's the beer guts.'

'What's going on?'
said Dad.

'We're going
to settle this nonsense
between you and Whacka
once and for all. In a peaceful
way,' said Mum. 'It's clear that
you can't live next door to each
other. Someone is going to really get hurt.

47

Either we go or they go. It's the only way. You're going to have a contest. And the loser will move to another house.'

'What about me?' I yelled. 'I don't want to move. Robyn is my best friend.'

'I like it here,' said Julie.

'Me too,' said Sky.

'I'm not going to a new school,' said Hayden. 'New schools are revolting.'

Jack didn't say anything. He doesn't even go to school yet.

'Anne and I have decided on a competition,' said Mum. 'And the loser has to sell up and go and live somewhere else.'

'What sort of competition?' growled Dad.

'You and Whacka are going to lose those beer guts,' said Mum. 'In exactly three months there is going to be a weigh-in. Whoever is the lightest is the winner. The other one and his family have to move house.'

Dad gritted his teeth. I thought he was going to say no. 'Good,' he said. 'A duel. Whacka will never

48

be able to stop stuffing his face. This time I'll really teach him a lesson.'

'Yeah, said Chris. 'We'll show him.'

Mum went and fetched Whacka and Anne over and everyone shook hands. Dad and Whacka wouldn't look at each other but they agreed that the weigh-in would be in three months time.

Dad gave a false grin with his false teeth. 'I'll win easily,' he said. 'I'll cut down from five beers a day to three. That'll do the trick.'

'I'll be your coach,' Chris said. 'We'll train every day.' My heart sank. Dad was never going to win like that. But either way it didn't matter. I would still lose my best friend no matter who won.

I went outside and sat on the footpath with Robyn. We were both upset.

'I always think that I'm a bit big,' said Robyn. 'There's nothing wrong with that, is there?'

I shook my head. 'That's just you. Dad and Whacka drink too much beer. And they eat too much junk food. That's why they've got pot bellies.'

'I don't mind a few vegies,' said Robyn. 'But why would Dad want to steal a cabbage?'

'Beats me,' I said. 'We all hate them. Especially Julie.'

'And now we're never going to see each other again,' said Robyn. 'All because of a cabbage.' Her eyes filled with tears.

She didn't want to leave either. What a friend. Both our hearts were breaking.

7

Chris's heart was not breaking. He was enjoying being Dad's coach. 'No beer until it's over,' he told Dad. 'And you only eat at meal times. No snacks.'

'No beer?' said Dad.

Mum and Chris both shook their heads.

So that was it. Fruit for breakfast. Salad for lunch. Nothing for tea. No grog. Dad moaned and groaned. But he stuck to it. He was worried. He didn't want to move either. And he didn't want to lose.

Chris looked out the window. Whacka cycled by. Yes, cycled. He was exercising on a bike. Robyn told me that he had taken a month off work. He was going to exercise and train all day every day.

'I can't do that,' said Dad. 'We can't afford it.'

Every morning Chris woke Dad up at five and took him jogging. At first it was one kilometre. Then two. In the end it was up to twenty. Gradually Dad started to lose weight. Half a kilo. A whole kilo. Two kilos. His trousers started to hang loose and he had to buy new ones. He was getting back to his old self.

'You look terrific,' said Mum. 'It's doing you a world of good.'

'Whacka looks terrific, too,' Chris said. 'His beer gut has almost gone. Dad will have to do push-ups every night or he's going to lose.'

Dad hung his head.

'And after that he'll have to do laps of the pool.'

Dad looked as if he was going to pass out. 'Okay,' he said. 'Let's do it.'

Well, it went on like this for three months. Train, train, train. Push-ups. Chin-ups. Squats. Skipping. Weight-lifting. Diet, diet, diet. Carrots. Celery. Tomatoes. Cabbage (bought from the shop). Apples. Oranges.

One night Chris caught Dad sneaking down to the fridge and eating ice-cream. Chris took it from him and gave him a stern lecture. 'You have to stick to the diet,' he said. 'You have to win. Even if it means giving up ice-cream and beer.' Dad nodded sadly and walked slowly back to bed.

8

Finally the day of the big weigh-in came. Dad went up to the bathroom for one last check. 'Seventy-five kilos,' Chris said. 'Have you been to the loo?'

Dad nodded. 'Don't worry,' he said. 'I've squeezed out every last drop.'

We all trooped outside. The whole eight of us. Whacka's wife Anne had put up a tent on the front lawn. The whole cricket club was there to support Dad. And the guys from Rotary had come to cheer for Whacka. Mr Richards from down the street was the umpire. They trusted him because he was in the cricket team and Rotary as well.

Robyn and I sat up the back. We knew that we didn't have much more time together. Robyn had tears in her eyes.

'Don't worry,' I said. 'We can always write to each other.'

Robyn looked at me. 'You're my best friend,' she said. 'Life just won't be the same without . . .'

She never got to finish the sentence. The big weigh-in was starting.

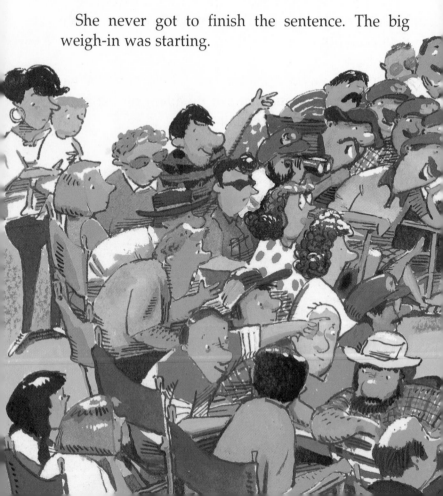

Whacka walked out with a towel wrapped around his waist. A big cheer went up from the Rotary guys.

There was a screen for Dad and Whacka to walk behind as they had to weigh themselves in the nude.

Chris's eyes nearly popped out of his head. It was hard to believe. Whacka's beer gut had completely vanished. He looked thinner than Dad. And he wore a huge smile. We were going to be the ones to move.

'After you,' said Dad.

Whacka walked behind the screen and gave a little speech. As he spoke he waved his hands over his head like a boxer. 'I've trained hard,' he said. 'I've eaten wisely. I'm the lightest and the best. You can kiss Johnny boy goodbye.' Then he dropped his towel and stepped onto the scales.

Mr Richards peered at the numbers. 'Seventy-four kilos, nine hundred and ninety-six grams,' he said in a loud voice.

A great cheer went up from the Rotary guys.

Whacka was four grams lighter than Dad. We were going to lose by four grams.

A hush fell over the crowd as Dad stepped up for the weigh-in. He walked behind the screen and dropped the towel to the ground.

Dad stepped towards the scales. It was all over. He was going to lose. We would have to move into a different area.

Poor old Chris. He was as white as a sheet. All that work. The running. The training. The advice. The early morning runs. All for nothing. His lips were trembling. He didn't care about moving house. He just wanted Dad to win. They were such good mates. I felt sorry for Chris. After all, he was only a little kid.

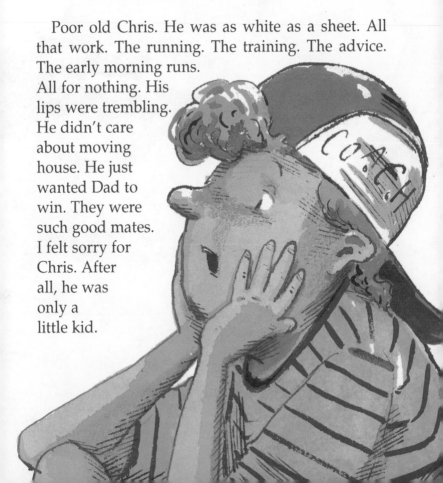

Suddenly Chris thought of something. 'Yes,' he yelled. 'Yes, yes, yes.' Chris rushed up to Dad and whispered in his ear. I could see that Dad was terribly upset. He bent down to listen and then started to cough and splutter into his hands. Then he straightened up. He shook hands with Chris and stepped onto
the scales.

Mr Richards
looked down.
Everyone was silent.
'Seventy-four kilos, nine hundred
and . . .' He bent down to look
at the scales more closely.

'NINETY-FIVE GRAMS.'

A huge cheer went up from the cricket club. Dad had won by one gram. Everyone rushed forward

and patted him on the back. It was a very happy moment. Mum's eyes nearly popped out. She didn't know how he could have lost the extra five grams. Neither did I.

'Robyn will have to move,' I said sadly.

'Terrific,' said Sky. 'We don't.'

Hayden looked at Dad's white skin. 'Revolting,' he said.

'We did it,' shouted Chris. 'We won.'

'How did he do it?' said Mum. 'I just don't get it.'

Jack didn't say anything at all. Neither did Julie. She just looked upset.

Dad and his supporters came back to our place for a barbie. There was no smoke coming from Whacka's yard this time. We had won. Now Whacka would have to move. So would Robyn and Anne. Whacka had to keep his word. The war was over.

Mum stood on a chair and peered over the fence. 'Look at this,' she said.

We all climbed up and stared into the garden. Whacka was standing there with his arms around Anne. They were both crying. They didn't want to leave their home. It was so sad.

Suddenly a voice piped up. 'Dad,' someone said. 'I have to talk to you.'

Dad looked down at Julie. 'It was me,' she said.

'What was you?' said Dad.

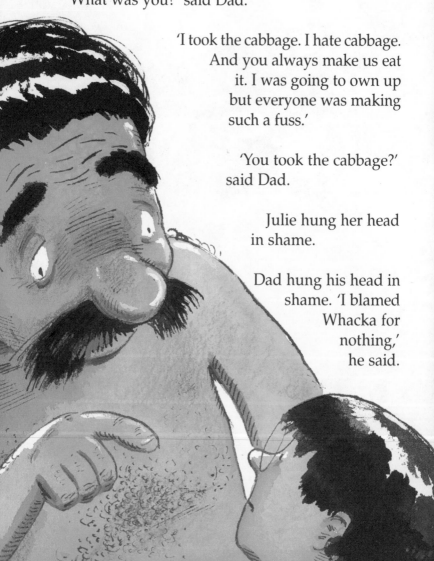

'I took the cabbage. I hate cabbage. And you always make us eat it. I was going to own up but everyone was making such a fuss.'

'You took the cabbage?' said Dad.

Julie hung her head in shame.

Dad hung his head in shame. 'I blamed Whacka for nothing,' he said.

9

Dad and Mum looked at each other. Mum nodded her head and Dad jumped over the fence. He was pretty nimble now that he had lost so much weight. He held out a hand to Whacka. 'Put it there, mate,' he said. 'You don't have to leave. It was all my stupid fault anyway. I'm sorry I blamed you for taking the cabbage.'

Whacka stared at Dad and then he held out his hand and smiled. 'You beauty,' he said.

'Come over and join the party,' said Dad.

Robyn and I just hugged each other. We were so happy.

Chris looked up at me. 'He is a great bloke, is Dad,' he said. 'Kind to everyone.'

Whacka and Anne came over and joined the mob. So did the Rotary crowd. It was the best barbie ever. Whacka ate fifteen sausages without stopping.

'That must be a world record,' Chris said.

Dad put down the barbecue tongs and looked at Chris hungrily. His mouth was all wrinkly. 'Have you got something of mine, Chris?' he asked. 'I feel like a feed myself.' He gave his moustache a bit of a lick and smiled.

You couldn't see his teeth.

'Wow,' I said.

'Disgusting,' said Julie.

'Fantastic,' said Sky.

'Revolting,' said Hayden.

'So that's how you did it,' said Mum. Jack didn't say anything. He's not old enough to talk yet. He doesn't even have any teeth.

Everyone's mouths just hung open. Chris fished around in his pocket. Then he pulled out Dad's false teeth. The ones he had taken from Dad just before the weigh-in.

Chris looked up at Whacka. 'They weigh exactly five grams,' Chris told him with a grin.

'Exactly five grams.'

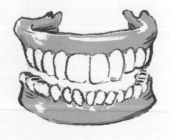

MORE GREAT READING FROM PUFFIN

☆☆☆☆☆☆☆☆☆☆☆☆☆☆☆☆☆☆☆☆☆☆☆☆☆☆☆☆☆☆☆

ALSO BY PAUL JENNINGS

The Cabbage Patch Fib   Illustrated by Craig Smith

When an embarrassed Dad tells Chris that babies grow out of cabbages, Chris searches the vegetable garden – where he finds a baby. Being an instant father is okay for a while, but Chris soon tires of parental responsibility, until his problem is solved in an hilarious way.

Winner of the 1989 Young Australians' Best Book Award (YABBA), Victoria.
Winner of the Canberra's Own Outstanding List Award (COOL), ACT.

The Paw Thing   Illustrated by Keith McEwan

The stomach of a cat is no place for a miniature radio, especially when it is switched on. A takeaway chicken shop is not the ideal home for a million mice. And 'Dead Rooster' is not an ideal name for a takeaway chicken shop. But in this crazy story you will find them all.

Winner of the 1990 Young Australians' Best Book Award (YABBA), Victoria.
Winner of the 1991 West Australian Young Readers' Book Award (WAYRA).

The Gizmo   Illustrated by Keith McEwan

Some gizmos are pretty weird, but this one is the weirdest ever! And it won't go away. A wacky new story by the amazing Paul Jennings.

The Paul Jennings Superdiary

When is a diary not a diary? When it has jokes, quiz questions, fan letters and lots more from Paul Jennings, including a brand new, full-length, really horrible story!